First edition for the United States, Canada,
Australia and the Philippines published 1988
by Barron's Educational Series, Inc.

First published 1987 by Walker Books, Ltd., London, England

All inquiries should be addressed to:
Barron's Educational Series, Inc.
250 Wireless Boulevard, Hauppauge, NY 11788

Library of Congress Catalog Card No. 87-16780
International Standard Book No. 0-8120-5885-2

Library of Congress Cataloging-in-Publication Data
West, Colin.
One little elephant.
Summary: As an elephant is joined by others, one at a time
the reader may count from one to ten.
[1. Elephant—Fiction. 2. Counting]   I. Title.
PZ7.W517440n   1988   [E]   87-16780

ISBN 0-8120-5885-2

Printed in Hong Kong by Dai Nippon (H.K.) Ltd.
789   9685   987654321

One Little Elephant

Colin West

CHILDRENS PRESS CHOICE

A Barron's title selected for educational distribution

ISBN 0-516-08561-1

One little elephant
Wondering what to do,

Once there was an elephant,
And then there were . . .

Two little elephants
Surfing on the sea,

Once there were two elephants,
And then there were . . .

Three little elephants
Singing at my door,

Once there were three elephants,
And then there were . . .

Four little elephants
Learning how to jive,

Once there were four elephants,
And then there were . . .

Five little elephants
Doing funny tricks,

Once there were five elephants,
And then there were . . .

Six little elephants
Think the beach is heaven,

Once there were six elephants,
And then there were . . .

Seven little elephants
Trying hard to skate,

Once there were seven elephants,
And then there were . . .

Eight little elephants
Skipping in a line,

Once there were eight elephants,
And then there were . . .

Nine little elephants
Snoozing now and then,

Once there were nine elephants
And then there were . . .

10

Ten little elephants
Playing in the rain,

Once there were ten elephants,
Let's count them all again . . .

Ten little elephants
Have had a lot of fun . . .

Once there were ten elephants,
But now their tale is done!